Praise for

THE MEMORY OF MARBLE

"...has the quality of an exquisite mathematical equation"
Fiona Capp on the story 'Temperament'.

"An amazing story, really arouses the tactile responses of the reader. My fingertips tingled"
Ania Walwicz on the story 'Cocoon'

"...proposes complex inner states of human consciousness through simple objects and the conglomerates of everyday life...This is the kind of domestic drama that reaches the proportions of the unknowable universe."
Ania Walwicz on the story 'The Clock Collector'

"shows sensitive understanding..."
Colleen Geebel, Judge of the Sunshine Coast 7th Annual Short Story Competition

"Imaginative...and beautifully developed"
Lyn Hatherly Wilson, Judge of the Mount Isa Annual Literary Competition

CAROLYN BEASLEY grew up in the bayside suburb of Altona, Victoria and now lives in a coastal town with a fellow writer and Bob, the shaggy brown dog. Her short stories have won many awards and her work has been published in Australia and overseas. She teaches writing at Swinburne University.

Her passions include sitting in gardens and staring at the ocean.

THE MEMORY OF MARBLE

THE MEMORY OF MARBLE

Carolyn Beasley

Lighthouse

First Published by The Rockview Press in 2006

National Library of Australia
Cataloguing-in-Publication entry:

Beasley, Carolyn.
  The memory of marble.

  I. Title.

A823.4

First Lighthouse Edition.

Typeset in Garamond

Cover design © Lighthouse 2018
Printed and bound in the USA

Dedication

To my darling sister Nicole for her calm words, vision and endless patience.

To my parents for never letting a day pass without kind words, encouragement and chocolate.

'The Memory of Marble' is a collection of ten stories that examine the boundaries we create between passion and obsession. The people in the stories seek refuge from emotions by cocooning themselves in the worlds of books, pianos, art, and fingerprints. A dying man imagines he can smell the history of graveside monuments, a fresco restorer battles madness as his diseased skin appears on the paintings he loves, and a blind book collector's world collapses when he discovers an insect incubating on a page. They inhabit arcane worlds that explode with sensation and sensuality.

Contents

'Skin's Rebellion' won 1ˢᵗ Prize in the 1999 Mount Isa Annual Short Story Competition, Open Section, under its original title 'The Painting Hand'. It has previously been published in the 1999 Mount Isa Annual Short Story Anthology and was commended in the FAW's Hastings Regional Literary Competition (Sails Resort) Awards that same year.

Skin's Rebellion

Skin's Rebellion

When restoring the images on plaster known as *fresco*, a thin layer of simpora revives the rose hues of the skin. The hand that applies it must be without quiver if the paint is to return to its original colour. If the paint senses even the first ripple of a tremor, it will crack in protest. Decomposition then begins.

Until this day, Luc's fingers had never twitched. He had worked on thousands of paintings and frescos, both in the cities where painting was born and in countries where it had been forced to sleep for decades. Through all this time, his hand had never caused a painting's death.

Using his right hand, Luc immersed the brush in a jar of water on the trestle table and then dipped the tip of the bristles into the bottle of simpora. Bringing the brush to the Madonna's fingers, he applied a gentle stroke along the curve where the Madonna's skin met her nails. The stroke had to be like a caress; slow, lingering and gentle. He waited for the colour to rise.

Gabriel, the artist working on the fresco beside him, came to stand by Luc's side. 'My God, look at the colour coming up from beneath the varnish!'

Luc lifted his left hand and held a finger next to the Madonna's. 'It needs more orange.'

'You get her skin tone by comparing her flesh with your own?'

'That was how Giotto painted.'

Gabriel glanced down at his own hands. They were stained with grime. 'Why are your hands so clean?' He peered down at Luc's palette. 'What are you using?'

'Simpora.'

'What?'

'It's my own mixture.'

'You're not using what the restorer told us to?' Gabriel's voice echoed off the high ceiling of the cathedral.

'This gets a better result.'

'Does he know you're using this?'

'I'll tell him when I've finished.'

'You are mad! He'll fire you. Within the hour you'll be sitting at Florence airport waiting for the next plane home.'

Ignoring him, Luc applied a dab of orange varnish to the Madonna's fingers. In all the years he had been mixing his simpora, he had never been dismissed. The senior restorers were always angry when he would not reveal the recipe, but they had kept their word not to speak of the substance. If the world knew of his mixture, it would be replicated and applied to the great works of art with much disaster. There was no hand steady enough to revive the tones except his own.

There were six apprentice restorers working on the wall of frescos that day. They were forced to place all their tools and chemicals on the same table. That, to Luc's mind, was the cause of the accident. It had been ten years since he was an apprentice and a similar number since he'd shared a workspace. Luc was used to his own carefulness and forgot that others have more harmful traits.

From the corner of his eye he saw a strange bottle but was so concerned about keeping the orange to the right shade that his mind dismissed it. As he turned back to the table, the edge of his smock caught the top of the bottle and knocked it over.

Brush still in hand, he reached over and caught the bottle before it hit the floor.

The chemical inside was an undiluted acid with the scent of lemon. The splashes on his left hand were pleasant at first, like the coolness of an aftershave to the cheeks. The sting had begun seconds afterwards, and then numbness as the pores had closed in shock and trapped the chemical in their wells. It was with the numbness that the flesh began to corrode. Blisters rose on the epidermis like mountains. Their weight grew so great that they collapsed inward, creating great craters like dormant volcanos that dipped deep below the surface.

Beneath the smell of his skin's death were the sharp top notes of the acid's lemon scent. Amid his screams and the scuffle that went on around him, Luc swore he saw the scent atomise and drift into his nose where it branded itself onto the lining of his smelling sense so that it and it alone would be with him always. From that moment on, all fragrances but lemon were memory.

Although they had rinsed his hand beneath running water quickly enough to save most of the nerves, it was the skin that told of the pain. For a month the decayed flesh had to be hidden from the air. He wore bandages wrapped like a turban across his knuckles, gauze like fishnet between his fingers. The surgeons had told him the deepest layers of the skin had been damaged, but it was not until his hand was released to the air that the horror of their words struck him.

The back of his hand had been replaced by a patchwork of hardened mounds, not quite scars, but too textured and raised to be considered blemishes. If they had been flesh coloured, he might easily have adapted to them. Like the figures in relief on a coin, they could have passed unnoticed except by touch.

But they weren't flesh coloured. They were a furious red, with edges as deep brown as an overripe pear. The knuckles at the base of the digits had merged into a ridge that spanned the width of his hand like the metal knuckle-dusters he had seen in his youth. His fingers looked as if an animal had gnawed the skin away, eating the soft folds at the joints and leaving patches of normal skin like tiny islands amid a corrosive sea.

The surgeons told him that he should be grateful he still had use of the injured hand. But the remaining skin was tight now, stretched so taut over the bones that it felt about to split like old vinyl when he tried to clench his fingers into a fist. How fortunate, they had said, that the hand that held the brush was spared.

The moment the doctors left him alone with the hand he had hidden it in the bandages again and left the surgery. On the way home he had passed the shop of an old tailor. In the window were hundreds of gloves, each a different shade and a different material. He stepped inside and, in halting Italian, purchased his first pair of gloves. Alpaca, sheep's wool, leather, vinyl, furs in mink and sable were all laid against Luc's damaged flesh, but only the leather caused no irritation. Luc wondered if this was because it, too, had once been skin.

The doctors had instructed Luc not to use the hand during the four-week recuperation he had been forced to take from work. If the lesions were to breathe the vapours of paint and chemical astringent used by the restorers, the hand may give in to bacteria. Even a simple act like mixing his simpora could lead to the loss of more flesh and the remaining strips of skin. For nearly a month the simpora's ingredients sat, neglected and unmixed, in bottles in the cupboard of his hotel room. During this time, the newsagent's boy left magazines and books of the Madonna outside Luc's door. Luc clipped and collected the images with his good hand and spent his nights dreaming of the Madonna's skin.

In the twilight of the recuperation his hand grew stronger and the remaining skin curled protectively over the edges of the damaged flesh. Luc thought about creating his simpora again. For the mixture to rediscover the original tone beneath the Madonna's layers of neglect, its separate parts must be in complete harmony. These would take at least three days to bond, and a half hour in the cathedral to penetrate the brush. To go back to work by the end of the week he must begin blending today.

The recipe would depend on the number of tones required to reintroduce life to the Madonna's skin. He set out the ingredients on the hotel room's small bench-top and tried to visualise the condition of the Madonna's skin. How many shades below natural was she? His mind tried to recall the density of her pores, but he seemed to have no memory of them. Instead he focused on the varnish. After all, that was what collected the grime that changed her colour. Yet that too was lost to him.

The air in the room suddenly seemed too hot to breathe. He rushed to the window, flung it open, and then leaned out to soothe his lungs.

His eye could recall the appearance of the skin in every painting and fresco his brush had transformed in the previous four years. Why suddenly could he not remember the last he had touched?

He had little choice but to make the simpora weak. A diluted mixture would take longer to find the colour beneath the varnish, but it was better than applying too much. Too much would cause the paint to rebel.

Once the leather glove was on, he cleansed the pipette and beaker of dust, unscrewed all the bottles, and then lined them up in the order of pouring. The vinegar was first. His damaged hand took the pipette and drew a millilitre of the liquid. He released it into the beaker. His hand hovered above the rim.

The recipe for simpora had never been recorded. To commit it to paper was to risk discovery and reproduction. He had memorised the mixture so long ago that he no longer recalled it when blending the substance. His fingers had seized the memory and simply carried out the steps needed.

Yet his hand still hovered above the rim of the beaker.

He curled, and then flexed, his fingers. The scarred skin beneath the leather glove was stiff, but obedient.

Again, he willed the hand to measure out the next ingredient.

It could not.

Dropping his left hand to his side, he picked up a new pipette with the right. He dipped the pipette into a bottle of spring water. Two drops of water? The right hand was uncertain.

The pipette slipped out of his fingers and fell into the bottle of water. He picked up the bottle and threw it against the wall.

'It's to be expected,' the doctor told him that afternoon. 'The fingers have been inactive for a long time.' He helped Luc pull the glove over the flesh. 'The hand, if unused, forgets.'

The first day back he wore the gloves to work. It was a necessity. People he passed on the street and sat near on the train became transfixed with the corroded canvas that was his hand. It was only when he was at the fresco that he removed the gloves. He placed a pot on the workbench. Three drops of vinegar for one teaspoon of each of the other ingredients, all fixed by a base of gelatine and spring water. He removed the lid from the simpora and allowed a few minutes for it to be re-acquainted with the point of his brush.

Shopping receipts had helped him rediscover the recipe. By examining their dates, he could see how frequently each element had been purchased. From this, he had calculated the ratios between the ingredients.

Two of his co-workers, who had already begun work for the day, stopped by his section of the fresco to wish him well. Luc thanked them and was pleased to see that they had left his fresco untouched. He began with the Madonna's wrist. A thin wedge of pale brown representing a shadow from the sleeve of her drapery had begun to crack, the colour slowly evaporating from the wall through the fissures to the air. Oxygen would bleach it, shade by shade, until the pale brown had lost all its pigment and become as bland as putty.

With a steady hand, he dabbed the brush-tip of simpora on the Madonna's wrist and left it to tease the colour back. Still holding the brush at shoulder height, he lifted his damaged hand and let it hover a few millimetres from the back of the Madonna's hand. His eyes roamed across his hand for any trace of life-like tone. There was only the offensive, startling orange.

He pulled up his sleeve. Could the underside of his wrist give inspiration? But the skin was remarkable for its colourlessness. The only changes in its whiteness were the thin, barely visible, pale-blue tunnels of vein running deep beneath the flesh. This skin was without the hues of life. It had not faced the world in the way the skin on the hands and face had and so could not offer guidance on the appearance of real skin.

Perhaps he could study the hand that painted. Holding the brush to the fresco, he tried to see the different shades of skin. It was impossible. He needed to view the whole of the hand.

Left with no natural coloured skin, he could only create tone from the past, recalling its whites, beiges, browns, blues and oranges from a time when he had never thought to memorise them. He touched the brush to the shadow on the Madonna's skin again and stepped back to wait for a stronger tone to fight its way from beneath the varnish.

'Monsieur Luc Guerin, good to have you back!'

Luc turned to find Marc Noyaux, the senior restorer, walking past the line of painters toward him. Marc's eyes assessed the work of each artist as he passed their fresco. Luc took another step back and let Marc seek the Madonna.

Marc stopped beside Luc and stared at the fresco. '*Merde*! What have you done?' He moved close to the wall and dabbed a finger on the Madonna's wrist. 'What is this colour?' He snatched the brush from Luc and felt the bristles.

Luc looked at the brush in Marc's hand. The tip, heavy with simpora, quivered as a drop left its point and fell to the floor.

Marc seized Luc's sleeve and pulled him to the fresco. 'Look at what you've done!'

The brown of the shadow from the Madonna's cuff had deepened to a coal-pit black, the darkness seeping over the flesh of her knuckles and turning the pink and white tones murky. The blackness had bled, little streams trailing into the digits and running towards the nails. Somehow the edges of the black had turned an angry, merciless red.

Marc threw the brush to the ground, slid his fingers from Luc's sleeve to the damaged hand, and raised the hand in the air.

'You have painted your own skin, idiot!'

Luc looked up at his damaged hand, and then at the Madonna's. He saw a similar pattern of blemishes on both, the same offensive ridge across the knuckles. Just as his skin was eaten away, so the Madonna's had blistered and buckled.

He snatched his hand from the restorer's grip and fled from the cathedral, jamming his damaged hand beneath his smock as he ran out to the roadside. The restorer's voice echoed from within the cathedral. 'She is unsavable.'

A taxi idled before him, stuck in the heavy morning gridlock. Sprinting over the curb and darting between the stationary vehicles, he opened the door of the taxi and tumbled in just as it was about to move with the traffic.

'Florence Airport.'

The taxi lurched forward and his damaged hand, still beneath the smock, fell against his chest. The doctors were wrong when they said the hand that painted had been preserved. He lifted the smock and stared at the injured fingers. The hand that had restored life to dying flesh was not the one that held the brush. By eating away his skin, the acid had released a contagion that seeped from his pores and jealously infected what the hand was supposed to save.

A block from the cathedral the traffic grew congested again and the taxi slowed. Luc saw three businesses nestled together in a large two storey shopfront. A cake shop, a butcher and a photographer.

'Stop.'

The taxi swerved to the side of the road and parked by the gutter.

'Wait for me.'

He jumped from the cab and ran into the butcher's.

The shop was empty except for an old, white haired man hunched over a crank-handled grinding machine on the front counter. As the man struggled to turn the arm, the grinder squeezed mince through its blades into a large steel bowl.

In his flawed Italian, Luc told the butcher what he wanted.

Mince stopped flowing. The butcher's forehead creased. '*Che?*' A shoulder shrugged. '*Non ti capisco.*'

'Speak English?'

'*Non.*'

'*Parlez vous Français?*'

'*Français? Oui, oui.*'

'*Alors, allez-y, coupez-moi la main.*' Luc held out his hand.

The old man stood still for a few seconds, then backed away from the counter, shaking his head.

Luc reached beyond the grinding machine and grabbed a cleaver that lay at its base. '*Maintenant! Vite!*'

He leapt over the counter and held the knife to the butcher's throat. 'Cut off my hand!'

'*D'accord, d'accord,*' the butcher whispered, hands outstretched and palms raised. '*D'accord.*'

Cocoon

Cocoon

'What would a blind man want with books?'

'He collects them.'

'Why?'

There is a rustle of cotton. I interpret this as a shrug.

Kenny the bookseller and his male customer think that I am not listening, or that I am too far away to hear. But four bookshelves is not what I'd call a distance and the shop is narrow. Even the scrape of the customer's cuff on the counter carries.

My fingers run along the spines of jacketless hardcovers until I find a typeface I like. Today, I'm in the mood for a thin sans serif with deco curves. When my hand reads what I've found, I'm not surprised. Under 'F' there is an embossed copy of 'Tender Is The Night' by F. Scott Fitzgerald. My pointer finger traces little circles at the intersection of the 'T' in 'Tender'. Gold ink is denser than silver, its coverage more complete. The letters are smooth with no particle decay. The title, I decide, is printed in gold.

I open the book and lift it to my face. With a steady breath I inhale the scent of the page. The ink begins as a flood of grit, then tightens to a sting of gallic acid. I feel the pores in my nostrils compress. This tells me the printing date is pre-1960. Modern inks have more resin than pigment and are diluted with too much water to hold odour.

The identity of the paper unravels. Dust in the pulp makes my nose tickle; yet my sinuses relax as vanilla is released. The paper must be American. Only in America do they pulp the vanilla scented red gum for books. Australian manufacturers use eucalypts.

I am excited by what this means.

The book is rare. A first edition.

I pull two other books off the shelf. Their titles and authors don't matter. They are camouflage. Kenny the bookseller is a vendor, not a collector. He sets his prices not on the front page of the book, but on how much he thinks you desire it. The Fitzgerald among other books will not catch his eye, but buying it alone may alert him to its value.

The customer leaves as I approach the counter. Above the scent of paper, the shop smells damp. I picture round light switches, oval fuse boxes and rectangular windows that open like cupboards.

'How much?' I ask.

The bookseller rustles through the pages. 'Special price for you, Mr Bowen. Ten dollars for the lot.'

My fingers search and find a note with the dimension of a ten.

He bags the three books. I tighten my scarf around my neck, flick my cane to its full length and tap my way onto the street.

Eleven footsteps away there is a rubbish bin. I toss all the books— except the Fitzgerald—and travel the three hundred and seven steps to my musty terrace.

As I pass each shop, I feel the world of my street turn. The travel agent is shelving new brochures, the slap of glossy page against glossy page spilling through her doorway onto the footpath. My ears grow suddenly warm. She predicts the heat of Bali will be popular this month. From the shop three doors down, ink and the sharp spice of fear rush to my nose. A man receiving his first tattoo. In the background, there is the constant growl of the highway.

As soon as I am home, I lean against the door and run my fingers over the pages of the Fitzgerald. Bookmakers check the direction of the grain by holding the paper against the light. I must rely on the textures of touch. Beneath the imprint of words the grain is thick with clots of wood fibre, each short, hair-like and lying parallel to the other. I feel the knots in a tree's bark, the softness of the red gum. The paper is so dry it sticks to my fingers, and I begin to worry. Common pulp has a low pH, its acidity eating at the cellulose fibres until the grain is yellow and brittle. If the book is to last, I'll have to treat it.

My finger touches something hard.

A raised lump, coarse with tens of tiny ridges.

I circle it with my finger.

It is oval, as long as a five-cent piece, but only as wide as the prong of a fork. I tap it with the tip of my index finger and feel I have made a dent.

A cocoon?

I bring the book to my face and inhale. There is the coppery scent of blood and the warm, moist stench of decomposing flesh.

The ringing of the telephone interrupts my investigation. After placing the book on the wooden entry table, I take the call.

'Mr Bowen, it's Helen,' the voice says.

'What time is it?'

'It's only one o'clock. Listen, I have to tell you something.'

'Go on.'

'I can't do your housework any more.'

'Why not?'

'My mother's sick. The council has found someone new to help you. She'll be there between one thirty and two.'

I step up to the table and trace the title lettering on the Fitzgerald again. 'You were always here at two.'

'Don't be difficult. Half an hour won't matter.'

I think of the camphor smell of her clothes, the apple breeze of her hair as she moved through the house.

'Are you coming back?'

'I don't think so.'

The Fitzgerald is on the kitchen table when the new help arrives.

I open the door. Her perfume is oriental, musk layered with heady spices.

'Sorry I'm late. The traffic on the highway's hell.' She steps inside. Her breathing is so heavy I feel like I can hear the puff and squeeze of every crevice in her lungs. She slams the door behind her.

The wall above the door groans and cracks. I feel a rush of air. Plaster rains down on me.

There is a moment of silence.

I touch my shoulder and feel powdery flakes beneath my fingers. The room is suddenly thick with the mould-like odour of mushrooms.

'Oh God, I'm sorry,' she says. 'Here, let me get this crap off you.' She tries to brush the flakes from me, but I take a step backwards.

'No, don't touch me. I'll do it.' I shake my head and particles tumble into my face.

'That's old houses for you, I guess.'

'I guess.' This has never happened before, but I don't tell her this. Instead, I offer my hand. 'I'm Michael Bowen.'

'Oh yeah, sorry.' She takes my hand and squeezes it. 'I'm Louise, but everyone calls me Lu.'

Silence stretches between us again.

'I suppose I should clean all this up first?' she asks.

'Maybe later. Could you help me dust my books?'

'Books?'

I turn and walk slowly from the entry hall into the front room. She follows and I sense her pause under the door frame.

'Holy Smoke, you've got wall to wall shelves! I didn't know they published so many Braille books.'

'Most of them aren't Braille.' I pull a book from the nearest shelf and open it.

I offer it to her.

She takes it. I hear her flick through the pages.

'I collect them,' I tell her.

'Doesn't it bother you that you can't read them?' She slips the book back into its place.

'I read them once.'

'You weren't always blind?'

'No.'

I remember how letters on a page look, but then they were just lines. It's only now that I have no sight that I wish I'd taken more notice of the curves and stalks of typography. Braille is as dull as courier.

'The feather duster is behind you, leaning against the wall,' I say.

She begins to clean. The dusting sounds soft, as if the lambswool is just barely touching the books.

'You're more careful than Helen,' I say.

'Well, I figure if you've collected all these, then they must be worth something.'

'Helen dusted so hard she knocked the books off the shelves.'

Lu chuckles. 'Bet that upset you.'

'It did.'

I let her dust for a minute or two, then ask, 'Do you read much?'

The dusting doesn't pause. 'Now and then I borrow a book from the library. I can't afford to buy new ones. Not that I care, really. Old ones are nicer anyway.'

'They are, aren't they? Come into the kitchen, I want to show you something.'

She follows me through the house. 'Jeez, it's hot in here.'

I pick up the Fitzgerald and hand it to her. 'Tell me what's on the page.'

The room is silent for a second or two. 'God, what the hell is that?' she mutters.

I wait.

'I think it's an insect's shell,' she says.

'A cocoon?'

'Yeah, a cocoon.'

'What colour is the cocoon?'

'Brownish.'

'Are there any holes in it?'

'Holes? Um, no. But the side is kind of dented.' Her voice fades and I guess she is looking around the room. 'Give me a knife and I'll get rid of it for you.'

'No, no. Leave it.'

Her voice is strong again. I know she's looking at me. 'You want to keep it?'

'Why not.'

'Get real. You can't raise an insect like a pet.'

'At least it won't cost me much in food,' I joke.

'You don't even know if it's an insect. It might be one of those white tailed spiders—you know, the ones that make your flesh fall off.'

She has a point. 'Perhaps I'd better find a pet shop,' I say.

'There's one a few blocks from here. I passed it on the way.'

'Where?'

'On this street, about four intersections down, past the highway.'

The highway. I have never walked that far but I know that Princes Highway is six lanes wide, with two tram tracks running down the middle. I'm told it takes two pedestrian lights and luck to cross it. 'Can you drive me?'

'Don't you want me to clean the house?'

'You could do that when we come back.'

There is a rustle of cotton fabric as she checks her watch. 'I can only spend another fifteen minutes with you. I've got to start at another place in half an hour.'

'We'll forget the cleaning then. If we leave now we'll be back in time.'

'Not in this traffic. You'll have to go on your own. Now, if you want me to finish the rest of the house, I'm going to have to open a window. It's a furnace in here.'

'I'll open a window.'

While she removes the broom, bucket and mop from the laundry cupboard, I turn off the heater and try to lift the pane on the loungeroom window. It is jammed. I take a deep breath and heave upwards on the sill with my hands. The glass finally rises, but the wooden ledge breaks off and falls to my feet. I crouch down and cautiously feel the wood on the floor. It has splintered into tiny spears.

'What the hell was that?' Lu calls. Footsteps grow loud as she crosses the floorboards. I hear her inhale in surprise. 'This place is falling apart.'

I gather the pieces.

The moment Lu leaves, I pack the Fitzgerald in waxed cooking paper and slip it into a plastic Coles bag. I step lightly through the front doorway and softly close the door behind me. I listen for the crash of more falling ceiling and feel relieved when I hear nothing.

It takes me fifteen minutes to reach the furthest point I have ever traveled. The smell of lemon Mr Sheen on damp timber is the last scent I recognise on my street. The furniture maker is the corner shop looking out over the highway. Cars and trucks speed past so close that the breeze from their wheels whirls around me like a cyclone. I take a step back. The drag of their undertow flutters the bag protecting the Fitzgerald.

When the cars stop I take a deep breath and hurry across, holding the book tight against my chest. By the time I reach the tram tracks, the traffic is flowing again. It takes another four minutes until they return to standstill. I begin to cross, but still have not reached the gutter when the clicking of the pedestrian signal slows and stops.

Engines roar. I hear the surge of a truck's motor as it increases speed and shifts gears. I scurry to get to the roadside in time and leap onto the footpath just as a truck's horn tears through the air.

Inside the bag I hear the pages of the Fitzgerald rustle.

I tap my way along the footpath until I smell bird food. The yap of puppies and gurgle of water filters grow louder and louder until I can pinpoint the exact door that they lay behind.

The Fitzgerald tucked under my arm, I push open the glass door and feel my way to the counter.

The shopkeeper's aftershave is lemon and lime with an undercurrent of green wood. The soft roll of a ballpoint pen tells me he's writing on notepaper.

I unpack my book and present it. 'What's on the page?'

The pen grows still. 'Hang on while I get a magnifier.' He pulls out a drawer and rifles through it, then takes the book from my hands. 'It's a larvae still in its womb. My God, the line of type is actually printed over the top of the cocoon.' The book thuds onto the glass countertop.

'What's in there?'

'I dunno. Looks a little like a fly cocoon.'

'You said the print was stamped on it?'

'Yeah. Weird.'

'What letter?'

'B.'

Five minutes later I leave the shop with the Fitzgerald and a bundle under my arm.

'B for bug,' Lu laughs when she comes to clean.

'A fly is a beetle, not a bug.'

'Whatever.'

'Can you help me set up the incubator?'

'The what?'

'The incubator. So I can hatch the fly.'

'If it's in a cocoon, what does it need an incubator for?'

'The cocoon's dented.'

'Hey, isn't a fly a maggot before it's a fly?'

I hand her the plastic bag holding my purchases. 'You'll be able to tell me when you read the book.'

'What book?'

'The one I bought on fly lifecycles.'

'You want me to read a book on flies?'

'It's not very thick.'

She rustles through the bag and pulls out the book. As she settles into an armchair, there is a thud against the ceiling, and then the sound of slow cracking.

Plaster and paint chips flutter down onto my face.

The cracking gets louder. I hear a whoosh and feel my hair rise and then settle. A piece of ceiling that sounds the size of a watermelon lands on the floor near Lu's feet.

She rises. 'Look, you can see the sky!'

I unpack the pieces of the incubator and lay them out on dining table.

Half an hour later, the incubator is finished. It's the size of my fist. A dome of plastic covers a small piece of acacia bark. The shopkeeper suggested tearing the page from the Fitzgerald, but I refused. Instead, we'll have to wedge the cocoon from the paper and place it over the bark. A tiny generator operated by a penlight battery will keep the air at 26 degrees Celsius.

Lu picks up the book and chisels off the cocoon with a butter knife. 'Shit.'

I'm hovering by her side. 'What's wrong?'

'I broke it open.'

'Quick, put it in the incubator.'

'Hang on, where is it?'

My hands feel cold and slippery. I force myself to take a calming breath. 'What do you mean?'

'It's empty.'

'My fly's gone?'

'Something's eaten through the cocoon wall.'

'From the inside or the outside.'

'The inside, of course.'

'I wonder where it went?'

She laughs and tosses the knife on the dining table. 'Maybe it flew through the hole in the roof.'

'First customer of the day,' the bookshop owner announces as I walk through the door. 'Looking for anything in particular?'

'Just browsing.'

I have never been to this bookshop before. It takes me a few minutes to find where the shelves begin.

I run my hands along the books' spines. My fingertips suddenly sting and I stop at that book. The tingle on my skin means a high acid content on the paper. The book is old.

The pages are thick and the grain fibres so coarse that I feel I'm rubbing my fingers against sandpaper.

The pads of my fingers search the pages for lumps. I find none.

After going through twelve books without finding a cocoon, I leave and head for home.

I'm walking on the pavement six shops from the pet shop when I hear a car slow and pull up beside me.

'Hey, Mr Bowen.'

I recognise Lu's voice.

'What are you doing down here?' she calls through the open car window. 'I thought you never crossed the highway.'

'It's not that scary.'

'Want a lift back home? I'm going to a client a few streets from you.'

I consider the offer. The highway still takes nearly ten minutes to cross and I never seem to make it to the other side fast enough to avoid the traffic.

'No thanks,' I say and walk on.

The Memory of Marble

The Memory of Marble

The crunch of tyres on gravel made Andrew look up from his paperwork.

Emilio glanced out the window. 'Delivery.'

Andrew pulled out the box of purchase orders. 'But no marble's due in.' He began flicking through the receipts. 'No one wants imported marble any more.'

Emilio opened the door of the office and stepped out into the afternoon sun. 'It could be the special I requested a few weeks ago,' he called over his shoulder.

Andrew rose and followed Emilio over to the delivery truck. Sensing Andrew was a few steps behind, Emilio turned to face him. 'I'll handle it. Finish your accounts.'

'You ordered a load of marble? How the hell are we going to pay for that?'

'It's only one slab.'

'One slab? We can't do anything with one bloody slab.'

'I told you, it's a special project,' Emilio waved a hand in the direction of the office. 'Now go back inside. I want you to finish the accounts.'

The driver climbed out of the cab, walked to the back of the truck and began unbolting the tailgate.

Andrew folded his arms across his chest. 'Don't you want me to take a sample and test the quality?'

'I'll do it.'

'You don't know how to use the microscope.'

Emilio's hands clenched into fists. 'I said I'd test it. Just go inside!'

Andrew held up his hands, palms facing Emilio. 'Alright, chill out' He shook his head and returned to the office.

The driver handed Emilio a clipboard. 'One slab of white marble,' he squinted down at the handwritten order sheet, 'from Carrara, Italy?'

'That's correct. Unload it and put it in the shed over there,' Emilio pointed to a small tin storage room at the end of the drive. 'I'll need to test it.'

'The boss told me to give you a sample for testing. Said it could save me unloading the slab for nothing. Hang on, I'll just grab it from the front seat.' Before Emilio could protest, the driver had disappeared to the front of the truck. He returned a few seconds later with a thirty centimetre square of marble. 'Here you go.'

Emilio took the square from him and carried it over to the storage shed. After locking the door from the inside, he brought the small block of marble to his nose, closed his eyes, and inhaled lightly.

Marble, if untreated, is porous. Without the armour of a chemical seal, it is defenseless against the environment around it and the lives that are lived on its surface. Over his forty years of sealing and treating marble, Emilio had seen stone weep a salty sediment of tears and release red stains of pain drawn from men's feet. Technicians like Andrew claimed it was the movement of iron within the rock that caused discolouration, but Emilio knew that Andrew's equipment could not sense the marble like he did and certainly could not smell its history.

Before all other scents, the sweat of the quarry workers rose to Emilio's nose. From this, he could confirm the origin of the marble. The climate surrounding the quarry where the stone was cut could be detected from the acridity of the fume. The sun's simmering heat must remove the acrid base that turns sweat stale when it reaches air, for the smell of South European and African marble always held musk. In contrast, Norwegian stone offered Emilio's nose more of the sting of ammonia. The colder climes seemed to tighten the skin above the glands and, combined with the layers of clothing, suppress the release of sweat to the air. From the sample rose the scent of musk, so Emilio knew the stone had been quarried in the sunnier regions of Europe.

Then the other smells were released. The invigorating tang of full, juicy, ripe oranges. Their skins, unwashed, still held the gritless warmth that sunbaked earth gives. And then another scent drifted from the rock—the woodiness of red wine kept too long in the dampness of a cellar barrel. The Carraran quarry was cut from Italy's Valencia district, its marble living for centuries in the path of winds that blew down from the orange groves and rocky vineyards of the Canista mountains. The underground streams that teased at the roots of citrus trees and trickled into the veins of the vineyard stalks had given the marble its gentle, undulating capillaries of colour and quartz.

Emilio was distracted by a scratching at the back of his throat. The lung was protesting again. Before the hacking cough had a chance to begin, he exhaled sharply. He then stared down at the marble, satisfied. There was no doubt this sample was Carraran marble.

He carried the sample back out to the truck. Andrew was standing at the rear of the truck, talking to the driver. Emilio could make out Andrew's words.

'With the economy so screwed, no one's buying. Unless things pick up within the next six months, we'll go under.'

'What'll you do, mate?' the driver asked.

'Dunno. A lot of cemeteries are importing ready-made monuments direct from the European quarries. They'd need someone like me.'

'What about him?'

'Emilio'll probably retire. His lungs are shot from breathing in all the grinding dust.'

The conversation died off when Emilio reached the men. He offered the sample to the driver. 'This is fine. You can put the block in the shed.'

The driver gave Emilio the clipboard. 'Thirty-day account. Sign here.'

Emilio pulled out a pen. 'I'd rather pay now.'

Andrew threw up his hands. 'Are you nuts? This stuff must cost $5000 a square metre!'

Emilio signed the page. 'I'll write a cheque.' He gave the clipboard back and returned to the office.

He heard Andrew's voice from across the yard. 'Marble dust's settled in his head as well.'

The slab took up nearly the whole area of the shed floor and he was forced to leave the door open to accommodate a corner of the stone.

He laid down on the block and tried to inhale from the lung, but the tickling began. The hack rose up and tried to pull at his chest until his shoulders buckled and racked. His whole body vibrated from the effort of keeping the hack contained. Each time it rose, he could only hold it for a lesser and lesser amount of time before the mucus and blood would burst up from the back of his throat and out into the air around him. When he looked down at the phlegm and found only mucus and blood he was relieved. It was the spots of black sometimes accompanying the blood that terrified him.

He wiped the specks of disease from the marble and brought his face down against its coolness again. Leaving his lungs to their struggle, he sniffed the grain instead.

This time there were no oranges and no wine. Instead, there was the unbearable stink of putrefying flesh.

He jerked his face from the surface and tumbled from the slab to the shed's floor. His stomach rose and emptied on to the concrete. Only once before had he encountered this smell of skin and muscle slowly liquefying and seeping back into the earth. White marble like that produced at Carrara was scarce and local manufacturers had been known to pillage the cemetery for the milky headstones used last century. In the industry there were even rumours that some imported stone had been stolen from crypts in ancient mausoleums. His nose proved this to be true.

In the past, he had been able to use marble that had absorbed man's mortality. Once, Emilio had separated the two layers in a slab of Blue Pearl from Norway and the marble had released the smell of a man's death. Quickly, he sandwiched the layers together again so the smell couldn't escape. He had locked the marble in the shed for two weeks while he thought about what to do. The stone had been ordered for a funeral monument. It seemed wrong to lay a man's last odours on another man's tomb, but fitting that it be let loose amongst like smells. In the end, Emilio had decided to free the marble rather than death's scent. He laid the marble, unsealed, in the afternoon sun and let it absorb the aromas of life around it. Only when he was feeling joy would he walk over its surface. This was in the times when work was abundant, and if he arrived at the yard before dawn he would drag the slab out to let it feel the delicate beauty of a sunrise and then the bustling energy of commerce. Gradually the memory of the marble was crowded until the smell of the stranger's death was pushed so far back in history that it was barely a ghost beneath the nose.

But his project required the Carraran marble be scented with life, not death. And since he'd fallen ill, his senses had intensified. No amount of re-exposure would completely remove the traces of what the stone had absorbed. This slab, and the other three he had accumulated in the last six months, were to shelter his body beyond this life, so they must have no undesirable undercurrents. Once sealed, they would replace the stench of his flesh's decay with the aroma of their memories.

A shadow fell across the marble. Emilio glanced up to find Andrew standing in the doorway.

Emilio wiped the back of his hand across his mouth. 'Return the slab. It doesn't come from the Carraran quarry.'

Andrew was silent.

Emilio looked up at Andrew again and saw that the younger man was staring at the concrete floor. Following Andrew's gaze, he realised the floor was covered in specks of blood and mucus.

Andrew knelt down beside Emilio and put an arm around his shoulder. 'Are you alright?'

Emilio shook off Andrew's arm and staggered to his feet. 'I'm fine. Return the marble and tell them I want a Carraran slab within two weeks.'

Andrew rose as well. 'I'm taking you to hospital.'

Shaking his head, Emilio kicked the block of marble. 'It's this that made me sick.'

'No, this is more than an infection from the dust. There's too much blood.'

'That's not what I mean.' Emilio scrambled past Andrew and out of the door. He took a shaky breath of air.

Andrew bent over the stone and stroked its grain. 'What makes you think this isn't from the same quarry as the sample? The ripple is the same. There are no spalls, open seams or pits on the surface.'

'It doesn't have the scent of Valencia.'

Andrew lowered his head to the slab and sniffed loudly. 'Can't argue with that.' He straightened up and joined Emilio in the sun. 'Just smells like rock to me.'

The truck returned in six days with a slab that the driver promised was Carraran stone. Emilio ordered that it be unloaded into the foyer of the office and then sent Andrew down to the barn.

'There are three slabs I want you to seal.'

'We have three slabs stored in the barn? What the hell for?'

'Something I'm working on. Keep them in the barn when you seal them.'

'But they need to be in the sun to dry.'

'No, the sun will affect the character of the stone. Be careful with them, they're heavier than normal slabs. Don't rest them against the wall.'

He listened to Andrew whistle while he gathered his sealing equipment. In all the years Emilio had shared with marble, he had never whistled or sung as he worked on the stone. Only in silence could the marble tell of the years it had absorbed.

Emilio told the driver to wait by the truck until he had tested the new delivery.

The marble held the same fine grain of quartz and sediment as both the sample and the previous slab. He lay along its length, smiled when he saw it stretched a few inches beyond his feet, pressed his face to its cold surface, and then took in its scent.

Decaying flesh, again.

He quickly lifted his face from the stone.

This was absurd! Were they stupid?

He rose and took a shaky breath. His chest constricted and he could feel the fluid from his lung rising to the base of his throat.

With a stab of panic, he realised his disease would claim him before another slab could be ordered and delivered.

The high notes of Andrew's voice drifted through the open window. Emilio scuttled around the slab to the door and called for him.

Andrew appeared at the office door immediately.

Emilio tapped the marble with the toe of his boot. 'Help the driver to shift the marble back on the truck.'

'What? You've got to be joking?'

'Please.'

Andrew shook his head slowly. 'You're losing it, mate.' He turned around and beckoned to the driver.

The driver leaned back against the truck and folded his arms across his chest. 'I'm sick of this. You clowns move it yourself.'

Andrew rolled his eyes, squatted down beside the stone's edge, and heaved the slab onto its side.

Emilio put a hand on Andrew's shoulder. 'Wait, it's too heavy. I'll get the trolley from the back room.'

Andrew shook his head and dragged the slab backwards out of office and into the yard. He rested it against the side of the truck for a few seconds, and then slowly let it fall against his shoulder.

Emilio watched him for a moment, then picked up an old paperweight made from Queensland black marble and bought it to his nose. He closed his eyes and gently inhaled, trying to ignore the sound of Andrew's deep breath of resistance against the weight of the slab.

Unconcerned, Emilio waited for the heady presence of the Queensland quarry workers to rise.

But again the smell of bacteria and dying skin.

Emilio slowly opened his eyes and stared down at the paperweight. This rock had come from a quarry fed by a millennium old rainforest. How could the marble have forgotten the lush carpets of damp moss that had seen man's life begin? How could it release instead the odour of coming death?

A new thought struck him. The paperweight slipped from his hand and fell back to the table. Perhaps the stench of decay was the disease claiming his smelling senses. What then would become of his Carraran crypt?

The sudden scuff of slipping gravel beneath shoes made Emilio pause and then glance up.

Andrew's feet were obscured by a white cloud of dust, but Emilio could see the muscles of his thighs tight against the material of his trousers, straining to resist the crushing weight from above. As the dust cleared, he watched the marble slab rock against Andrew's body, forcing his feet to slide further out from under him each time it contacted with his shoulder.

Emilio felt his mouth form a cry, yet his ears registered no sound except the scraping of feet against gravel. Andrew's eyes shifted to Emilio's and held them as the marble pushed him to the dirt and then absorbed his bones with the slow crunch of fossil under a boot.

The driver and Emilio rushed to lift the stone, but it was too heavy.

Emilio threw himself to the ground and tried to wriggle beneath the slab to pull Andrew free. The marble accepted his left arm and leg, but no more. He reached out and grabbed Andrew's shoulder.

'Oranges,' Andrew spluttered. Blood created new grain against the whiteness of the stone. 'I can smell oranges.'

'The Garden' was Highly Commended in the Fellowship of Australian Writers' Far North Coast Regional Literary Competition in 1999 and Highly Commended in the Mystical Flight Literary Competition of 1999.

The Garden

The Garden

The day after my brother died, my grandmother phoned and asked me if my mother had been crying.

I said no, I didn't think so.

The next day she called and asked again.

I told her to wait while I ran and asked my mother. My mother stormed to the phone and told my grandmother to mind her own business and not to call again.

Three days after my brother died, my mother moved into the garden.

She crept back into the house after we'd all gone to bed, at least I guessed she did because there was nowhere for her to sleep out back and she'd never been the sleeping bag type. It wasn't as if she'd made a decision to avoid my father and I, it was just that the wilderness of weeds that she'd let creep up to the house held promise for her.

So she traded cooking our dinners with mixing fertiliser, helping me with my homework with attending to root rot. While the weeds were steadily replaced with jasmine, daisy bushes and golden diosmas, I lost four kilos and Dad's nightly tinkers in the garage grew to four hour engine demounting sessions. Soon we had a garden full of perennials and the smoothest running cars in Cranbourne.

The neighbours started asking me if they could show their guests the garden, and soon the local primary school was holding regular excursions into our street, down our front path, through the side gate and into the back yard.

My mother became a figure I saw through the windows of the house, a hose in one hand, a small trowel in the other, floppy hat protecting her face from the sun. Sometimes I saw her squat down in front of a new, unopened bud, take off her leather glove, and caress the tightly clenched petals. I swear I even saw her talking to them, her eyes closed, lips barely moving. It was the way the bud swayed as her shoulders rose and fell that told me she was whispering to it.

By the third month Dad had all but moved into the garage, entering the house only to change clothes before running back to his car and disappearing under it or slipping his head beneath the hood.

One day I missed the bus and had to walk the five kilometres from school to home. I cut through an industrial side street and walked past a small nursery that I'd never noticed before. Lined up on the pavement outside the entry door were three small pots of white flowering bushes for fifty cents each. Mimicking my mother, I lifted the leaves and checked the underside for bugs and discolouration, then stuck a finger into the soil to check the moisture level. I picked the plant with the most new buds and carried it into the shop, standing on tiptoe to set it on the counter. I paid my fifty cents and then proudly carried the plant home.

When I arrived my mother was arranging tanbark around a new daisy bush. I carried my purchase out of the house and placed it on the porch by the back door. I got a trowel from the shed and began digging a hole near the back fence, in one of the few vacant patches of the earth, between a sprawling carpet rose and an enormous, flat topped diosma.

She heard the digging and slowly turned around, dropping a handful of tanbark to the ground when she saw me on my knees, ploughing into the earth.

'What are you doing?' she demanded.

I rose and fetched my plant from the porch. She stared at the pot in my hands and then back up at my face.

'I bought it. It's mine.'

She shook her head angrily. 'You can't plant that!'

'Yes I can. I watched you. I know how.'

She nodded toward the plant. 'No, I mean I won't let you put that thing in my garden. It's a bedding begonia'

I stared at her.

She tried again. 'It's an annual. It only lives for one season.'

'You can make it live.'

She rushed over to me and pulled the pot from my hands. 'No. No one can make it live longer than that. It'll die within the year.' She walked over to the rubbish heap and tossed the pot in the bin.

I turned and walked back into the house.

By the next evening a large, white-flowered bush occupied the hole that I had dug. I watched as my mother gave the new addition a small amount of water, and then cleared the tanbark from the earth surrounding the base of the plant. She removed her floppy sunhat, lowered herself onto one knee, and leaned over the tallest shoots.

Whispering again.

I moved away from the window, went to my room and started doing my maths homework. I'd only completed two problems when I heard the sliding door that led from the lounge to the back yard travel along its railings.

Thinking my father was making a toilet trip, I kept jabbing numbers into my calculator until my ears told me the stride along the tiles was not my father's shuffle.

I lifted my head and listened to my mother walking slowly down the long corridor to her bedroom.

The door to my parent's walk-in wardrobe creaked and I heard the thud of objects being moved around in the closet. The thuds were replaced by the long, drawn out whisk of a zipper being opened.

Clothes hangers tinkled against each other for nearly two minutes and then the hasty whisk of the zipper again.

I rose from my desk and walked down the long corridor to my parent's bedroom. Without knocking I stepped into the room and watched as my mother snatched her old mid-sized orange suitcase from the bed and placed it by my feet.

'I'm going to the holiday house for a few days.'

I said nothing as she pulled out Dad's old, tubular golf bag and tossed his clubs on the bed. Dissatisfied with my response she looked up at me. I stared at the empty golf bag.

'So I can carry the gardening shovel, pick and weed remover down with me,' she explained.

My hole in the ground had been one of the last free spaces in her garden. Now that it was full, I suppose she had to find another garden to grow.

She crossed the floor to me and grabbed my shoulders, eyes trying to reach mine for the first time since she'd moved out of the house. 'You'll water the garden while I'm gone?'

I continued staring at the golf bag.

She shook my shoulders. 'You'll water the garden while I'm gone?'

I finally met her gaze. 'Yes.'

'Good. Once a day only. In the evening, only after the sun has almost disappeared. No earlier or you'll burn the roots. Any later and you'll attract bugs.'

I returned my gaze to the golf bag. 'How long will you be gone?'

'I said a few days.'

'How long is that?'

She exhaled impatiently. 'I don't know, okay?' She turned back to the bed, grabbed the golf bag and then slipped a hand through the handle of the suitcase. I stepped aside and let her pass through the doorway.

Her keys jangled as she picked them up from the entry hall table and let herself out the front door.

I returned from school the next day and went straight to my room to do my homework. When the sun started to dip beneath the line of the neighbour's fence, I packed up and went outside into the garden.

Mum had left the hose and the long armed sprayer coiled at the foot of the back porch. I stepped over them and walked slowly along the perimeter of the white garden beds, letting the competing scents wash over me, wandering down the length of the garden until I reached the line of trellising that hid the garden shed from view. I breathed in the sweet smell of the jasmine that scrambled up the thin chequerboard wooden planks and with the toe of my school shoe ruffled the tiny, star-like white flowers that had fallen from the vines to the ground. They fluttered into the air and settled back down on the earth a few centimetres from where they'd first been, revealing a tiny patch of dirt with a few blades of browning grass.

I squatted down and poked a finger into the uncovered earth. It was hard-packed and dry, needing water.

I leaned forward and felt the ground by the stem of the jasmine bush. The earth covering its roots was also parched.

I stood up and walked back to the porch, stepped over the hose, and went inside to cook myself some dinner.

The temperature during the three days that passed before my mother called was in the early thirties, with no cool change expected for at least another three days.

'Are you watering my garden?'

'You asked me to, didn't you?'

'But are you doing it?'

'Of course.'

'You haven't forgotten the apricot tree by the back gate?'

I forced exasperation into my voice. 'No, Mum.'

'How's your father?'

'In the garage.'

'He must be alright then.'

'When are you coming home?'

Silence. Then, 'Maybe the day after tomorrow. I've ordered a new lot of soil for the areas around the walls of the house. The earliest they can deliver it is two days from now.'

She hung up and I looked out the window to check the position of the sun. It was out of sight, maybe just below the fence line. I walked out to the patio, stepped over the hose, and walked to the nearest flowerbed. I forced my finger into the earth and wriggled it around beneath the surface. The surface of the soil around my finger cracked and broke up.

I walked back to the patio, stepped over the hose, and went inside.

My mother's car rolled into the driveway two weeks later. She pulled the golf bag from the boot and let herself into the backyard through the side gate.

I watched as she set the bag down by the garage door and hurried over to the closest flowerbed to inspect the condition of her plants.

She stared at the withering brown leaves and wilting buds—uncomprehending—for ten seconds then dropped down to her knees and, using her palms, lifted a low hanging branch whose petal heads had dipped down to touch the earth. The stems slipped from her hand and dropped back to trail along the tanbark. She stared around the rest of the garden, taking in each withering plant and scrub.

I left the house and walked up behind her. She rose slowly and spun around to face me.

'What have you done?'

'Things die, Mum,' I said quietly.

She grabbed my shoulders and shook me. 'Not here.' Her eyes grew watery. She suddenly dropped her hands from my shoulders and turned back to the garden. 'Not here. I won't let it.'

I wrapped my arms around her waist. 'Things die,' I repeated.

She broke free of my hug and ran inside, slamming the sliding door closed behind her.

Dad poked his head out of the garage door. 'What's going on?'

'Mum's garden's dying.'

He stared out at the yard. 'It's not dead yet. She can bring it back.'

I shook my head. 'It's too late.'

He dropped his gaze and disappeared into the garage.

I followed Mum into the house. Her sobs were audible from the moment I stepped inside. I started to walk down the corridor to her room, but the door was closed.

I turned around, went to the phone in the kitchen and called my grandmother.

'Mum's crying now,' I said.

The Temperament

The Temperament

Temperament: A system of compromises in the tuning of pianos.

Francis loves Balaclava because it is more a hamlet than a suburb. Cinnamon air from the bakery lures him from bed in the mornings, and on street corners bearded old men talk with their hands. People greet him by name on his way to his piano repair shop, just as they did his father and his father's father before him.

But it is 2006 and the walls of his shop cannot hold back the future. Piano makers cut production by 60 percent, the third last of Francis's customers chokes on a fig at the age of 91, and Francis's hand begins to tremor.

'Old Mrs Bloom died last night,' his assistant, Paul, says as Francis enters the shop.

'I know, I paid my respects to the family this morning. No one wants her upright Steinway so it's ours.' Francis glances at a box on the floor. 'Is that the part for the Bennett?'

'No. Can you believe her tree only gives one fig a year? What were the chances—'

'Ring the supplies and find out how far away that part is.'

'What's the hurry? Tightass Terry still owes us a hundred for the Bennett's last repairs.'

Francis opens the box. 'So what is this?'

'Sound board for Billy Webster's guitar. It's a 70's Gibson.' Paul grabs a note pad from the counter. 'What part were you after for the Bennett?'

'The hammer butt.'

Paul's pen floats above the page. 'But one came in a few weeks ago.'

'It was faulty.'

'A faulty hammer butt? From Bennett? That's a first.'

Francis's voice is firm. 'Please just order the part.'

'Okay, okay, keep your socks on.' Paul writes down the name of the part. 'You know, the guitar part there in the box is worth more than a week of tuning. Not that we've had that amount of business in a while.'

'I'll be in the workshop,' Francis says though his teeth.

As Francis dusts the outside of Mrs Bloom's piano, he marvels at its perfection. Two thousand moving parts, all crafted to produce variations of seven notes. At 65 years of age, he is a baby compared to the Steinway beneath his fingers. Yet he feels as old as the music it plays. Each event of his life is tied to a worn piano part. His first memory is touching a key. Beneath the old Wessell action that hung on the wall was his first and only kiss. His mother died as he replaced the dampers on a cheap Yamaha and his father was committed to the home after stuffing tuning felt down the chimney of a rival's shop.

And the first piano injured by the shake in his hand was a Bennett with a broken hammer butt.

He can't bring himself to tell Paul about the tremor. Paul is a kind young man and a good technician, but has no passion for the piano. With his shaggy hair and loud rock musician friends, he doesn't understand the joy of giving a string its voice back and the devastation of accidentally ripping that voice away. Paul would say the tremor means his hand has had enough of slipping into tight places and coaxing out sounds. But he has given his life to pianos. If he gives them up, what does he have left?

'Got you a tea from next door,' Paul says from the doorway. 'I'll leave it on the workbench.'

'Thanks.' He keeps working until Paul leaves the room.

The tea is cool. He wonders how long Paul has been watching him.

He lifts the plastic cup. Only a small waves slops over the side. The hand is having a good day.

He plays all the keys of Mrs Bloom's Steinway and listens for the rattle of foreign objects. Over the years he'd found enough strange things inside a piano to start his own museum. Children's toys, hearing aids, even a family's pet mouse. He hears the tremor of something on the soundboard at the bassest C and D. Lying across these strings is an old photograph of Mrs Bloom sipping tea at a table with his mother.

That Mrs Bloom knew his mother is no surprise. Balaclava was even smaller when his mother was alive. She would help his father organise community concerts. What surprises Francis is how happy his mother looks. She is not yet broken by a man with temper like a string too tense, ready to snap.

Francis has always blamed his mother's death on his father's passion for recitals. Like Francis, she was round and soft with small feet and longed to live in pianissimo. Her husband, however, tuned both stringed instruments and his life to concert pitch. He could never say no to a violin, guitar, piano or viola. He lived for the hour before a performance when he alone created the instrument's signature sound, and lived again for the hand-wringing hours beside the stage waiting for something to go wrong.

Outside these times, he was impossible. In his shop, he would listen only to the applause at the beginning and end of live recordings. He would refuse to tune an instrument left in a sunlit room, refuse to start a meal until he could create a perfect note from the striking of cutlery. The house and the shop were graveyards of guitar necks, violin bows and skeletal pianos.

As her husband slowly went string mad, the wife took it all to heart. After a while, that heart refused to beat in rhythm. One day, it simply refused to beat at all.

When Francis took over his father's shop, the window was repainted to read: 'Piano Tuning and Repairs: Domestic and Small Halls Only.' Never, he swore, would he deviate from this. No concerts, no violins, no violas, and no guitars. Only pianos. The string sickness would stop there.

Paul appears in the doorway of the workshop again. 'The guy from the Traders Association dropped by to see if we're going to put a float in the Street Festival this year. I told him no.'

Francis gently closed the lid on the Steinway, then lets himself get annoyed. 'Why?'

'We can't afford it. Last year's float cost us about three hundred bucks and how many new clients did it bring us? None.'

'I tuned Albert Klein's baby grand six days later.'

'He booked two days before the festival! And for what good it did. He died six months after that and his son took the piano interstate.'

'We'll build a cheaper float this time,' Francis says.

'For who? The oldies that still have pianos are so bound up with arthritis they can't even lift the lid and all the kids want to play guitar these days. We're better off investing whatever money we've got left into guitar repair equipment.'

Francis folds his arms across his chest. 'The piano is due for a revival. I read it in the industry news. Prices have dropped. We'll make a float to remind people what a beautiful instrument the piano is.'

'Kids don't care about beauty. All they care about are screaming solos, looking cool and being rock stars. I heard the local high school are looking to buy six guitars. If we got in quick we could make a few hundred on the sale and get callback work on the repairs.'

Paul recognises the look on Francis's face. The obstinacy in the jut of the jaw, the way he does not look Paul in the eye. This is the expression he remembers on Francis's father. Paul knows his boss has already made up his mind.

Paul gives it a final try. 'It could fund your float in the parade.'

'You may be right about the float,' Francis admits. 'But there'll be no guitars.'

Francis removes the front top panel of the Steinway and begins working on the tuning pins. It's been six months since he last treated the piano. Since then the weather has moved from cold to humid, and the strings cannot remember if they should be slack or taut. They are out of tune.

He finds a reference point for the temperament by muting all strings but the three that make up middle C. He strikes this note and listens. The strings chime but there is a strange echo left behind. This is the pulse of a string too slack, the sound of a string that has missed its cue and joined the others too late.

Lately he thinks of himself as a string out of tune. A beat behind the world as it marches past. Paul is right about the financial problems of the shop. There are no new clients and the old clients cannot afford repairs. Something must be done.

With his tuning hammer, he tightens this string. When he strikes the key again, all three strings sing in unison. The beauty of this sound makes his heart tick like a metronome at andante.

The perfect note and his steady hand lift his spirits. Paul is right about needing to diversify. But why resort to guitars?

After releasing the mutes, he closes his eyes and runs his arm down the other strings. He can feel their slackness by the way they bow against his skin. When he removes his arm from the innards of the piano, his flesh is marked with arcing lines. The deeper the arc, the more tuned the strings.

A guitar would never speak to him this way.

He tunes an octave so that the upper tones are double the number of vibrations of the lower. This octave becomes the set of notes against which all others are balanced.

But the nature of the piano is that for some notes to have tune, others must not.

'A rose has thorns,' Francis's father would say, 'just as all fifths are too sharp and thirds too flat.'

Francis was never sure about that logic, but he flattened the fifths and sharpened the thirds anyway.

In the times of unequal temperament and before science was applied to music, technicians would simply leave the end notes out of tune.

Setting an equal temperament requires compromise between the ideal and the necessary.

Francis takes this thought home.

The next morning, Francis makes Mrs Bloom's Steinway the centrepoint of the window display. A 'For Sale' sign rests on the keys. He sprinkles flower buds and stems around the piano.

By the end of the day the 'For Sale' sign has fallen into the lilies he's arranged at the base. There have been no inquiries about the piano. No one even slowed as they passed the shop.

'For Sale, Free Lessons,' reads Paul as he enters the shop. 'Since when do we sell pianos?'

'You suggested extending our range of instruments.'

'I see the town's queuing up round the block.'

'A piano is not an impulse buy. It's like choosing a lover. Someone will pass each day, taking in a new detail each time. First, their eyes will settle on its physique. Nice colour, they think, great shape. Then they'll notice the way the leg curves and the mahogany highlights in the wood. I could wake to that everyday of my life, they think, maybe even show it off to my friends. They come inside to hear it play and are seduced by the smell of lemon oil on varnish. Touching the ivory keys reminds them something civilised can be found in wild places. They play and it sounds like it will only ever play for them. Voila, a match.'

'Very impressive. Any suitors so far?'

'People are noticing.'

Paul slaps a letter on the counter. 'Do you think we'll marry it off before the electricity bill is due?'

Francis stares at the amount on the bill.

Paul sighs. 'I didn't think so.'

A week later, Francis sweeps a dead fly from the window display and dusts the Steinway. He plays 'Fur Elise' during the street's lunchroom rush. The hand stays steady. Most people wave hello as they pass. No one pauses to admire the piano. The sign reads: 'For Sale, Free Lessons, Free Tuning'.

'Funny how the morning light makes old Mrs Bloom's Steinway look so black,' Paul says. He is unpacking ten guitars and checking their condition in his space in the workshop. It is his lunchbreak and the guitars are his own project. 'I almost thought it was a different piano.'

'I darkened the varnish so no one would recognise it,' Francis explains. He cannot bear to look at the guitars, upright and tall in their stands. They are like an invading army.

Paul looks up at Francis in surprise. 'Why bother? No one's noticing it anyway. And dark varnish attracts dust and collects fingerprints.'

Francis holds up the sign. Paul reads it and laughs.

'For Sale, Free Lessons, Free Tuning. Once played by Elton John.'

When Francis returns from his lunchbreak, the piano is gone.

'I sold it,' announces Paul.

'You sold it?' Francis can barely squeeze out the words. He switches his cup of tea from right hand to left.

'To a kid and his mother. The mother couldn't speak English and the kid asked who Elton John was. I said he was a friend of Jimmy Hendrix. He asked if Jimmy Hendrix had ever played it, so I said 'yeah, all the time.' He got his mother to write out a cheque on the spot.'

'It must have been that teenage boy who almost stopped at the window yesterday. I could see he was quite taken with the piano, but was too shy to come inside.' The tea is hot against his palm. He switches it back to his right hand.

'Sorry mate, but he was here to buy a guitar. I threw in the piano at a discount.'

'A discount?' Francis's lips press tight. 'You cut the price on my piano so you could sell a guitar?'

'No, no, it wasn't like that. He would have bought the guitar anyway. I thought that you wouldn't mind if I took a bit off the piano's price. Seduce them a little, like you said.'

'That's not what I meant. Why did the boy come here to buy a guitar? We don't sell guitars. We will not sell guitars!'

'Francis, you're going under. If you stick to piano repairs or even move into pianos, you won't be able to pay your own wages anymore. That Bennett part you wanted isn't even made anymore. That's how bad it is.'

Francis is so angry his body begins to shake. 'Damn you! How I run my business has nothing to do with you.'

'I'm going to sell guitars because guitars sell,' Paul yells back. 'If you won't let me do it here, then I'll open my own place.'

Francis watches helplessly as the cup rocks a few times, then crashes on the floor at his feet.

'Jeez mate.' Paul puts an arm around Francis's shoulders.

The hand shakes uncontrollably.

It is a month later. A teenage boy enters Francis's shop. 'The guy in the guitar shop sent me over here.'

'What for?' asks Francis.

'Smells Like Teen Spirit.'

This is the tenth copy he'll sell this week.

Francis directs the boy past the piano that has been in the window for two months. Paul crosses the road every week to help tune it. On the wall are racks of sheet music arranged according to style. Classical, Broadway, Jazz, Pop, and Rock.

All for piano, but with guitar tablature as well.

The thorns on the rose, his father would say.

A temperament, thinks Francis.

'Formaldehyde' appeared in issue No: 20, 2004 of 'The New England Review'.

Formaldehyde

Formaldehyde

'Be quick, she's waking up.'

Emily opens her eyes to find a man breathing alcohol at her face, pulling at the bag slung over her shoulder. She shoves the man away and manages to stand.

They are in a dark cobblestoned lane—she, this thief and the thief's two accomplices. The men are thick as cattle as they try to herd her against the wall.

She pulls out the tiny revolver hidden in her coat pocket and pushes it into the closest man's temple. He is suddenly still while his companions spill over chamber pots and garbage pails in their hurry to flee.

'Run,' she orders as she lifts the gun from his head.

He does.

She knows why she has been lying in the street. Her disease is like formaldehyde. It leaves foam on her lips and lulls her into sleep. Its only evidence is the soreness of her muscles and the tenderness on her tongue.

Emily slips the revolver back in her coat pocket and walks towards the noise of the main street. All the women she passes hang from the arm of a man.

Above her, there is the clunk and whirl of machinery. The lemonade squeezers are working late in their skeletal factory. The season for preserving lemons is nearly over. As soon as her lungs collapse around the smell she is delirious with memory.

In the flash of a second she remembers lying under lemon trees in her lover's backyard, cooling her teeth on pulp and rind. She imagines men licking the citrus from their wives' fingers, tongues nibbling for secret pieces under the curl of the nail. Longing tightens her chest.

As she wanders back towards her dark rooms by the bridge, cockroaches crunch underfoot. They come to the canals at night to feed on the docked garbage barge. She watches them scurry from the light and sees their backs rise as they climb over something by the water's edge.

Following them, she moves towards the sucking kiss of the tide against the shore.

She finds a wet violin, heavy with swollen wood. She wants to hug it against her chest, as mothers do to stop their babies crying. Her hands lose themselves in its varnished strangeness and little curves.

The feeling of formaldehyde drifts from her forehead to her eyes to her shoulders like a feather floating past.

Only the scent of lemon brings her back.

On her good days, she lectures in a secret room in the basement of University. Today, her audience is nearly all women. One man sits in the shadow of boxes at the back of the room. Cockroaches crackle as they scurry through discarded cellophane. Above this is the quiver of her voice.

'There are parts of the woman's body that are removed to restrict pleasure. But there are things that women add to increase pleasure. A hole in the ear is created to draw amorous bites. Lips are painted to simulate female sexual organs. Necklaces attract eyes to tendons of milky skin. Toenails are painted to draw attention to carefree feet.'

She has charts, diagrams, models with removable layers.

'Musical instruments are even created to mimic the female form. They are played, plucked, stroked, and held. But in public, only by men.'

The violin rests on a stand beside her.

The man stands up after she completes her lecture. She watches him cut through the crowd like an icebreaker's bow. She knows this type of man.

They share too many words to fit into a conversation. They leap like crickets from one idea to another.

The room empties. She imagines that he would leave a trail of lovers like spent runners in a relay. She imagines herself as his instrument and he as hers.

He admires her violin and plays for her for the first time. His music curls around her like smoke from a cigar. She closes her eyes and feels the formaldehyde haze gathering.

The music stops.

Only his touch on her hand brings her back.

'The Clock Collector' was Commended in the Sunshine Coast Writers' Group Literary Awards of 1999. It was first published in the anthology 'By Fair Means or Foul' in 1999.

The Clock Collector

The Clock Collector

Rose swore it was the break in the rhythm of the drips that woke her. The clang of the metal wrench against the water pipe was not loud enough to pull her from sleep, but the sudden absence of the two-year-old beat was like the shrill ring of an alarm clock.

She threw off the covers, swung her legs over the side of the bed and padded resignedly into the hall. He's here one night, she thought, one single night, and already things are how they were.

A thin line of light glowed from beneath the closed bathroom door. She stepped up to the door and leaned an ear against the large white plane of wood. She heard a soft curse and the crash of metal hitting the floor.

Rose sighed.

She pushed open the door and saw Mark lying on the floor, head and shoulders lodged between the doors of the cupboard beneath the vanity sink, water dripping onto his angular face from the pipe above him. A gentle stream of water crept its way from the puddle under his jaw down to the floor, steadily heading for the seat of his blue striped pyjamas. The large glass salad bowl she'd placed under the pipe to catch the drips was sitting, empty, on the small counter beside the sink.

Rose shook her head in dismay. 'Leave the tap and go back to bed, will you?'

Mark jumped at the sound of her voice, then peered down the length of his long body to look at her.

'Mum, how am I supposed to sleep with this stupid thing thumping all night? How long has it been dripping like this?'

'It's a recent thing.'

He picked up the wrench, manoeuvred it above his head and up against the pipe. 'Your water bill will skyrocket.'

'There was only a ten dollar increase.'

He began tightening the joint on the pipe, then paused. 'It already registered on the bill? You just said it was recent.' He went back to working on the pipe.

'Well, since you were here last.'

The wrench froze and he lifted his head to stare at her. 'Mum, it's been two years since I left for Hong Kong.'

'I'm used to the drips by now.'

He placed the tool by his head on the bottom of the cupboard. 'Why doesn't that surprise me? I always told Dad he should have let you fend for yourself more. He's been gone three years and you still haven't taught yourself to fix a leaky tap.'

'But if I'm used to the dripping, why bother tinkering with it?'

'You probably can't even hear it with all your clocks. Those bloody clocks, by the way, are almost as loud as the dripping tap.'

Rose's hands sprung to her hips. 'I turned the chimes off!'

He wiggled backwards out of the cupboard. 'Then turn the damned ticking off too. Thank God you didn't start collecting them when Dad was still alive. The ticking would have driven him mad as well.' He rose to his feet and then shook his head, forcing the droplets of water to spray into the air.

Rose stepped back into the corridor but little arrows of water hit her face regardless. She took a deep breath and tried to keep the irritation she felt with him from her voice. 'Leave the tap. I don't want it touched.'

He bent down, picked up the wrench from the bottom of the cupboard and gave her an exasperated look. 'Mum, it's keeping me awake!'

She rolled her eyes and stepped back into the bathroom, leaning past him and opening the mirrored medicine cabinet that was mounted on the wall above the vanity basin. She reached up to the top shelf and grabbed the highest box off a pile of identical small cardboard packages.

'Here,' she tossed him a box of earplugs.

He caught the box in his right hand, looked down at it and then stared into the medicine cabinet. 'Christ, how many packets of those things have you got in there?'

She slammed the door of the medicine cabinet shut. 'Go back to bed.' She held out a hand, palm up. 'And give me the wrench.'

Mark handed her the wrench, offended. 'It's not like I was going to flood the place.'

She grabbed the salad bowl from the counter and settled it into its place under the pipe in the cupboard. 'And I don't want you trying to fix things when you think I'm not looking.'

Mark rolled his eyes and went into the bedroom across the hall from the bathroom. 'If I don't sneak in a few repairs while I'm here this place is going to fall apart. Oh, and by the way, you don't need the bowl,' he called as he closed the door behind him. 'The tap's fixed.'

She turned back to look at the bowl under the sink. Sure enough, it was still dry. She left it there anyway, switched off the bathroom light and went back to bed.

She lay in the darkened room, waiting for sleep to nestle upon her. The clock she kept by her bed had exhausted its battery a week after the tap's first drip. She had intended on replacing the battery straight away, but the drips had filled the silence left by the absence of ticking. Now, without the measured rhythm of the tap's dripping, the seconds and minutes lost their demarcation, each stretching into hours.

She gave up and flipped on the bedside light to consult her wrist watch. Only ten minutes had passed since she'd returned to bed. Eyes roaming around the room, she noticed the orange carpet had faded to a mustard by the window, broad paths rubbed into the pile where feet had gradually compressed and parted the fibres. When had the cracks that webbed out from the top of the walls appeared? The cream paint along the skirting boards peeled away? It dawned on her that perhaps Mark was right. The house was falling apart.

She rose and tip-toed down the hall, past the guest room and into the lounge beside it. She pulled the door closed behind her and leaned against it, closing her eyes and letting herself be engulfed by the gentle ticks that flowed from every corner of the room.

Making time real.

There had seemed to be no end to time when Bert was alive. Nothing aged, at least nothing seemed to. The changes that age had brought upon Mark and Bert were subtle, undetectable because they had occurred day by day, every day. They had only jumped the canyon etched by years in photographs. In her mind, in mirrors, they and herself were unaltered. When Bert was alive, even the house had been timeless, unchanged for the forty years he had lived here. But a month after Bert has passed, the flap on the letterbox broke. When she looked closely at it, she saw one of the hinges was newer than the other and that some of the screws were a different size to the original ones. It was then that she realised her memories of timelessness were a lie, because to look unchanged everything must have been replaced.

So she had begun to collect the clocks, their tick the reminder that time passed with each movement of the cog, that she was one second closer to reuniting with Bert. The ticking and the tap's drips helped her measure out the duration of each moment.

Now that the dripping had ceased she'd have to move one of the clocks into her bedroom if she wanted to get any sleep. She opened her eyes. But which one? They were all show clocks, most over a hundred years old, either far too heavily cased or too mechanistically delicate to withstand the journey down the hall. She stroked the turreted caddy top on the English Longcase and ran a finger along the curve of the French glass-plated, skeleton clock.

A thump echoed from Mark's side of the wall. She heard the bed springs complain as he shifted his weight restlessly.

An irony, she thought, that he couldn't sleep because of the clocks, either.

Leaving the clocks, she stepped into the corridor and stood outside the guest room. After a second or two she gently opened the door and looked in. Despite the dark she could see the open box of earplugs on the dresser.

The bed had been pulled into the centre of the room, away from the wall shared by the lounge. Mark lay on his stomach in the bed he used to sleep in as a child, but he was now so tall that his toes hung over the edge of the mattress. The pillow rested over the back of his head and was squashed down around his ears. The tick of the clocks were nearly as loud as in the lounge.

She backed out of the guest room and returned to the lounge. Starting with the English Longcase by the door, she moved to each clock and stopped it. Many, she suspected, would have to be serviced before they could be started again. When the room was silent she went back to bed.

Unable to measure the time, she concentrated on her breathing, using it to regulate the silence around her. In between breaths her ears searched for any rhythms that the clocks and dripping faucet had obscured.

Soon the silence faded and she began to hear the world outside the house. She grasped for a regular beat in the distant growl of the freeway and the hum of the electricity that ran the street and traffic lights. But they were constant, offering no break to distinguish one moment from another, the past from the present.

Then underneath the continuity she heard a new noise. A cricket's pulsing vibrato with intervals that were sometimes uneven, but intervals nonetheless.

She listened for a few seconds, then minutes. Smiling because she knew she had listened for seconds, then minutes.

Her eyes closed and she slept.

'The Violin' appeared in the October/November 2004 issue of *'Polestar'* magazine.

The Violin

The Violin

Gabriel died in the fifty-second bar of Wisemuller's Symphony.

I knew it was the trill that did it.

He always feared his hand wouldn't jump from note to note with the nimbleness demanded by these never-ending semiquavers. Fingers had to dart like cockroaches over the violin's neck. Every morning of his performing life, he claimed to wake with knuckles stiff from terror. While his mind slept, his index finger and left pointer would beat the pillow until they broke through the fabric and felt the scratch of the stuffing beneath. Tired of spending a wage on manchester, his wife switched from white linen cases to swirling coloured designs. These accepted fingerholes with discretion.

The fear of the imperfect trill haunted Gabriel even during daylight hours. He laboured his fingers to numbness four times a day to achieve the appearance of effortless semiquavers. Yet in every performance his hand still trembled at the last note of the fifty-first bar.

On the floodlit stage of Festival Hall, seated with four other violinists at the front centre of the orchestra, we began the long strokes that anticipated the trills of the Symphony. As we moved through the fifty-first bar, my eyes rested on Gabriel's hand. Music must be played by time signature, not personal prompt, but the quiver of Gabriel's fingers as they approached the fifty-second bar was so reliable I always set my rhythm by it.

I waited for his tremble.

The elbow of his bow arm rose and lingered in the air. His fingering hand was still. I had played the symphony with him for over a decade and knew there was no pause. He tumbled forward to the wooden floorboards of the stage, left hand still clutching his violin to his chest. I heard the snap of catgut.

The orchestra played on for two more bars.

'Gabe!' Cradling Gabriel's head in my arms, I watched his chest labour to rise and fall. Words he spoke to me years ago floated through my head. A silent violin, he'd said, is as sad as death.

I lowered my lips close to his ear and hummed his part.

He lifted the violin from his chest and thrust it at me. 'Save her.'

We'd met on the hottest day in Melbourne's history. People spoke of hot winds stealing water from goldfish bowls and of eucalypts bursting into flames. The cockroaches gathered under dishes and glistened like oil slicks. Gabriel fled the shade of his house, he'd said, to escape the exploding glass of its cheap thermometers and the maddening flutter of his wife's hand held fan.

On days this hot, the barber shop was the only place to be. In the heat of intolerable summer nights we all dreamed of reclining back in the barber's old dentist's chair with an icy face cloth clamped over our jaws. Ignatius's Cutting Salon was always popular in the hot season because it had the good fortune to be the property that separated the iceworks from the beer distillery. Being there was like sitting in a fridge until 4 pm, when the iceworks switched its generators to low. When we arrived home at 4.30 our wives thought we were sniffing for dinner like faithful dogs. It was simply that after 4 the barber's grew as hot as anywhere else. So it was here, early on Sunday afternoon as my quartet played, that Gabriel arrived.

As Gabriel waited for Ignatius to finish giving old man Hennessey a shave, the barometer above the door swung from Hot to Hell.

'Last shift at the iceworks,' Ignatius said without taking his eyes from old man Hennessey's face.

Gabriel watched the clock and my quartet played on. Five minutes later at exactly 4 pm, heat pulsed in beneath the door, fluttered the straw blinds and layered against our skin.

We all exhaled in unison and our breath charged across the room at Ignatius like a cannon shot. The blade slipped from his fingers. Old man Hennessey's skin parted and began to drip. The air was so hot, the blood dried before it hit the floor.

My E string snapped at the next bar and the brazilwood of the bow groaned as it forgot to breathe. It could only sweat.

Gabriel ruffled through his pockets and presented me with a small white packet. Inside was a thick coil of catgut.

'An E', he announced as he took the violin from my arms and began to restring. 'I can't bear the thought of a silent violin. It's like a death.'

I watched him work. 'A new string will be impossible to tune in this heat.'

'Tune it from mine,' he said as he tightened the pegs at the end of the fingerboard. He gave me back the violin and pushed into the heat of the street to fetch his own.

We tuned our violins to a common pitch and played in key for twenty years.

For three days following Gabriel's death, the violin stayed close to my heart.

The first day after Gabriel's death I displaced one of my own altos so that his could rest on a stand in the music room. For half an hour, I loved her in order to grieve. Running the heels of my hands around the swell of her curves, letting the skin of my cheek fill the grooves left by the whiskers of Gabriel's chin. With my tongue I tasted the salt his fingers had left on the strings and felt the channels his fingerprints had etched in the fretboard. Slowly, the wood swelled with the water of tears. She grew so heavy I was forced to play her flat against my chest instead of under the chin. I discovered it was true that violins held against the heart keep the tightest rhythm.

On the second day it was the violin's turn to grieve. All songs except requiems caused broken strings. Stale air stilled the vibration of her sound box until resonance was lost. I retreated from the room and left her to her pain.

On the third day my wife woke me early. 'That thing in the music room had better shut up.'

I stumbled to the music room and rested an ear against the door. I've seen men strike piano notes simply by singing into the string box and I've heard a cello imitate its owner's soprano during a summer storm. But never before that moment had I heard a violin call its master's name.

From beneath the door slipped a 'G' so low I felt its rumble shake my diaphragm.

And then the long drawn out semibreve 'A' Gabriel used to tune the second string.

Next, a 'B' so high I winced.

The final note an 'E', as angry and harsh as the bow jerked across an open string.

'It's just the weather,' I assured my wife. 'The heat makes the strings contract.' But I had heard the letters as clearly as if they'd been spoken.

So had my wife. 'Get it out of my house.'

I charged into the room, snatched the violin from the stand, and packed it away in its suede-lined case. I made a show of putting it on the front porch. As soon as my wife left for her evening visit to her mother, I brought the violin back into the house and hid it beneath the linen in the hall cupboard.

That night I called every violinist I knew.

One by one they all declined.

'Gabriel Auteil's violin? The one that played his death? Thanks, but I could never strike a note without thinking of him.'

'Performing in a dead man's instrument? You must be mad. I won't touch it. Sell it anonymously to a music shop.'

'Burn it. Bad juju.'

'Don't forget your violin, sir,' the porter called as I stepped out onto the street.

I had chosen the wrong hotel. The Lamont was not grand enough to attract thieves.

'Thank you,' I said and accepted the boxed instrument from his outstretched arms. I hurried into a taxi before the porter had time to demand a tip.

'The Savoy' I announced as I placed the violin on the floor behind the driver's seat. When we were only an intersection away from the Savoy I offered the driver twenty dollars. 'Here will do. Keep the change.'

I leapt from the taxi, wove through the other vehicles and disappeared into the crowd.

The violin and my wife were waiting inside the door when I arrived home.

'The Savoy dropped this in,' she said.

'But how-'

'A taxi driver brought it to the hotel and the Concierge found Gabe's name engraved on the backplate. He looked in all the café's until he found Gabe's wife. She told them to bring it here.'

'Good Lord.'

She shook her head in disgust. 'Put that thing in the garage before it starts again.'

In the dull light of the garage, I cut each string from its tuning peg. Finally all four were lying limp in my palm. I could see four long lines, like shadows, stretched along the fretboard where they had lain.

Like ghosts, I thought as I locked the violin in the garage cabinet where I keep my instrument parts.

I dream sometimes that the violin disappears and finds a life under someone else's chin. When my wife wakes, she says she dreamed it was playing at the shore of the canals. Every few months I unlock the cabinet just to check it's still there. It always is, but still we dream.

The Fig

The Fig

I think it was the day our fig tree bloomed that Sam decided to leave me. When I look back and try to pick the moment when it all came undone, my memory seems to jam right there.

We were all standing beneath the tree—the two of us, the kids and the dog. A branch near the top had us mesmerized. It was a late spring, still so cool that the sunflowers I'd planted the season before were too confused to blossom. The neighbours were listening to Midnight Oil again, and in the distance I could hear the rhythmic thump of someone practicing drums in a garage.

That crazy Craigieburn wind rocked our back gate against the fence so hard the latch broke.

'Gates gone again,' I said.

'I only fixed it last week,' Sam said.

'Well, better fix it properly this time,' I joked.

The fig tree was old, with branches as splintered and curled as a cinnamon stick. The tree gave only one fig each year. Sam always said it was the pH of our soil.

That day, however, he said more.

'It's bitter, lifeless soil. Dead from being all used up,' he said, giving me a sharp look that took me by surprise. He walked to the shed.

I tried to understand the words and his look. A nasty tone could slip out without provocation. If a day felt too long or too hard, a voice could shorten or twist into a snarl. But words like his took a long time to build up, even longer to be spoken. Maybe that look had started a while ago, but I'd never noticed.

Confused, I stared at his back until he disappeared into the shed. When he returned with the ladder, I kept my eyes lifted to the fig.

He climbed up and untwirled the little white hairnet that we'd wrapped, cocoon-like, around the fig. That, a flapping white plastic bag, and a little scarecrow James had made from ice-cream sticks stopped the birds eating it.

Sam passed the fig down to James.

'Jen, I'm sorry. I didn't mean that,' he said when he'd climbed down.

'It's okay,' I said.

That's when I began to watch him.

Every year, I divided the fig into thirds to stop everyone fighting over it. But the fig was always tiny so its pieces were no bigger than a slice of cherry tomato. And the kids always argued over the piece that was the biggest.

That year was no different.

'Danny, give that one to your father,' I said.

'But he doesn't even like figs.'

Sam got up from the table. 'Jesus, Jen, give it to him or we'll never have any peace.' He took a beer from the fridge.

James tried to grab a sliver that had fallen off Danny's piece. Danny punched him on the arm. James started to cry.

Sam shook his head sadly. 'Look at them, they've spent the last two weeks waiting for the thing to fall off the tree and what do they get? A bite the size of a ten-cent coin and a punch-up.'

'That's life,' I laughed.

Sam stared out the window and watched the dog urinate against the fig tree.

I wondered what he was really seeing.

Sam was always a restless sleeper, but that night I noticed his insomnia for the first time. The space beside me was cold and empty when I woke at 3am. The emptiness felt familiar and I realised it had happened before. I just hadn't really noticed. The sound of the television bounced down the hall.

We hadn't argued for a long time, not since he'd stopped working nightshift a month ago. Things were supposed to get better when he changed jobs and worked days. We'd see each other. Be more than shadows that swapped places at 7.30 in the morning. Live in the same time zone for once.

I got up and joined him in the lounge.

'What's on?' I asked.

'Dunno.'

'Can't sleep?'

'Well I'm awake, aren't I?'

'You worried about something?'

'Naa. Just can't sleep.' He turned to me. 'Don't you ever just get tired of everything?'

'Everything? Like what?'

He stared at the screen again. 'I don't know, of doing things for everyone else.'

'Of course.'

But he wasn't finished. 'It's like you and that bloody fig tree. Every year it's the same, you never cut any fruit for yourself. As if you don't deserve any. As if you always have to come last.'

'Don't think about it like that. It's just a fig.'

He nodded but I could see he wasn't listening. 'Go back to bed, Jen.'

'It's not that I come last, it's just that you guys need some things more than I do. When you do things out of love, you don't worry about coming first or last.'

He sighed. 'Okay then, you go on to bed. I'll be there soon.'

I lay awake listening to the sounds of the television. He's just going through a rough spot, I told myself. A few months ago they'd installed a new computer network at the Mint where he was a hardware technician. If it wasn't working properly it could hold up production for days. That was a lot of pressure for a thirty-eight year old man to carry.

Yet he hadn't been working late like he did when the machines were down. And he'd always let off the steam with me, not at me. So things must be okay at work. Anyway, we'd always had good talks when things were not going well. When my mother died, he'd found a book about life after death and read bits aloud to me. When James was diagnosed as having asthma, we'd stay up late nights working on a management plan. When Sam quit his job maintaining computers overnight at the Stock Exchange, we spent that afternoon promising each other we'd never work jobs we hated.

We hadn't had long talks like that for a while. In fact, I realised, we barely talked at all now. There was always something to do—get the kids ready for school, sport, dinner, or bed; maintain the garden; finish off the work from the office that we'd had to take home. I'd always thought of us as doing these things together. Just as I'd assumed that there was nothing we needed to talk about.

After all, who could find the time to be unhappy?

During the next few weeks, I tried to notice things. I listened to every word I said and the way I said them. I tried to see myself in his eyes and to hear myself with his ears. I listened for too much hardness and then for too much softness. I tried talking less, then talking more. I tried to listen for hidden meanings behind what he said, but he said too little for me to analyse. I asked him what was wrong, if he was still sick of 'everything', but he snapped that 'everything' was fine. He said I worried too much.

Growing desperate, I checked Sam's address book for new phone numbers and his little pocket diary for strange appointments. Nothing had been added.

Still there was the emptiness beside me in the early mornings.

Two months later, Sam announced the Mint were sending him to Darwin. A new security device on the hardware that needed a specialist's hand, he said. It'll only be for a few weeks and we could do with the money.

I realised it had already been decided.

Maybe this is what he needs, I thought, a bit of adventure.

Some time away from us.

And 'everything'.

We drove him to the airport on a rainy Sunday. James cried at the Departure Gate.

Danny punched him on the arm. 'Baby!'

Sam patted James on the head. 'I'll be back soon.'

Three weeks later, during one of his weekly phone calls, Sam told me his contract had been extended.

'Why don't we just move over there?' I asked. 'I could get work anywhere. We all need a change, anyway.'

There was silence.

'We could rent out the house. The company pays for your accommodation there. We could all squeeze in to your flat.'

There was nothing but the buzz of the phone line between us.

'Sam?'

'Sorry, Jen, but I'm not coming home to you.'

I could hardly breathe. 'What do you mean?'

'I can't live like this, Jen. I'm not like you. I can't wait for good things to fall off trees. I'm tired of having to give up everything, of having to work all the time for everyone else.'

'You mean for us?'

'Yes, and for the house and the car and bills.'

'But you're not the only one who works for those things. I work to pay for things for you and kids too. That's just something that has to be done.'

'That's what I mean when I say I'm not like you. I can't do it anymore. I can't...' His voice cracked. I could tell he was crying.

'Quit your job then. Come home. I can work longer hours for a while so you can have a break.'

'You do enough already. You don't need another person to baby and feed.'

'But you can't leave the kids.'

'And what about you?'

'I'm not worried about me.'

'That's exactly what I mean. You haven't missed me, have you?'

'Don't be stupid—of course I have.'

But he was right. I wasn't worried about him leaving me, I was worried about how I was going to feed the kids on one income.

Why didn't I miss him? What was wrong with me?

'We're dead, Jen. We've got no life left in us anymore. You can live like that because looking after the kids and paying the bills *is* your life. You're always looking ahead, but you never look around. I need to look around for a while. I need to live.'

The next year's fig appeared as a tiny green bump in the middle of a branch.

That same morning my car wouldn't cough to life.

I joined the queue at the bus stop and waited.

The bus crawled through back streets I'd never driven down before. It was still dark, but as we passed through the old part of Craigieburn I noticed that driveways were lit up with truck headlights. It felt wrong to be getting up with the truck drivers, as if I were just a small part of a machine that no one noticed.

I put my face to the window and tried to make out the houses as we passed. The ones with trucks were the best kept. One truckless house had a rusty drum of paint nailed to a wooden post for a letterbox, a few others had sheets over the inside of the windows. Another, a brown brick box the same size as our place, had an old car battery sitting against the fence. The fence was broken at the gate, just like ours.

I heard the hum of traffic moving down the Hume Highway.

We snailed our way into a new area. The houses here had verandas, garages and rows of standard roses.

I decided I didn't want to catch the bus anymore.

Every morning, my neighbour Ted steered his Cortina into our driveway.

'I got a new batch of fertilizer,' Ted said after he'd parked his car beside mine. 'Maybe you want to put some on your garden. On that fig tree of yours.'

'Don't you want it for your own garden?' I asked.

'Not much growing this season. I can see your fig tree from my sunroom. It's looking a little sad, to be honest.'

'There's no point—we only get a fig a year.'

'That's cause you don't treat it. A bit of nitrogen fertilizer and you'll see a few more. By the way, it should be fruiting twice a year.'

He hooked our cars together and yelled at me to turn the engine over.

My car droned a few times. Finally the engine roared.

'I'll drop that stuff over the fence for the kids,' he said as he wound up his jump leads.

'Ted, if I paid you, would you do a bit of maintenance around our place? I hadn't noticed how much I've let things go.'

'Tell you what, I'll help you for nothing if your kids give me a hand. Frankly, they should be pulling their weight a bit anyway. I mean, with your husband gone and all. Let you have a bit of a life.'

When I got home from work, I found the kids in the garden. Danny was shovelling fertilizer from the bag to the base of the tree. James smoothed it over with a piece of cardboard. Ted was hanging over the fence, instructing.

'What's with the frogmen?' I called from the back step.

The kids wore handkerchiefs over their mouths and swimming goggles.

'Stay back, Mum, it's toxic,' James called.

'Meet our OH&S rep,' laughed Ted.

'How long until the smell goes?' I asked.

'A few days,' Ted said. 'But you'll notice it a bit when it rains.'

'Ted, why don't you come in for dinner and a talk when you're done?' I said.

'I don't want to disturb you.'

I smiled. 'Don't be silly. It's the least I can do.'

'Okay. I don't bother much with cooking since Christina died.'

'Then I'll give you some to take home.'

After Ted left, James put four pairs of socks on the kitchen table. 'I need new ones,' he said.

'Why?'

'They've got holes in them.'

'I'll just sew them up.'

'You already did.'

'Oh?' I picked them up and examined the toes.

'The other end,' he said.

I looked at the heels. They were ripped.

'My school jumper has a hole at the elbow too.'

'That we can definitely fix,' I said.

He says nothing.

I realise that it's been a while since I've spoken more than a few words to him. 'How's school, mate? When does your cricket team start playing?'

He bundles his socks up in his arms. 'Mum, are we poor?'

'I don't know,' I said, 'maybe. Does it feel like we're poor?'

He thought for a minute. 'No. Poor people don't have food, right?'

I hugged him. 'We'll always have food. Do you want to help me fix the gate?'

'Can I paint it to make it look nicer?'

I wondered how much paint cost. I decided it didn't matter. 'Of course.'

A month later James came running into the kitchen.

'Mum, come and look at the fig tree.'

'Why?'

'Just come.'

I followed him into the garden. The fig was still wrapped up in its little hairnet. It was nearly all brown.

'Yep, that's ready,' I told him.

'No, not that. Look at the other side of the tree.'

I followed his pointing finger. On the opposite side of the tree, a little higher up, was a tiny green bulb.

'Another fig?' I laughed in amazement. 'We've got another fig!'

'See Mum,' he said seriously, 'all we had to do was feed the tree. Dad always said it just needed a bit more life.'

'When did he say that?'

'The year he left. I asked him why we couldn't just give the tree something to make it better, but he said it was too late to change anything.'

'Looks like he was wrong.' I nodded towards the shed. 'Use the ladder to pull the first fig down and then I'll cut a piece for each of us.'

'But I thought you didn't like figs.'

'I might try a piece this year.'

A Fingerprinter Falls In Love

A Fingerprinter Falls In Love

I'd fallen in love with Alex's fingerprints two months before I met him.

After my transfer from Perth to Melbourne, I was kept off the streets for a week and introduced to the geography of my floor—job roster on the whiteboard in the operations room; prints recorded on index cards arranged in drawers marked by the year the impression was taken; the login details of the computer networks; and the layout of the laboratory. My desk was a three-legged table with faux silky-oak grain laminate. Three plastic crates took the place of the fourth leg and camouflaged a sticky black stain on the brown carpet that smelt like sour milk. From my chair I had a view of the men's toilet. If the door was left open, I could see the urinal.

I found Alex's prints in the lab. Catherine was pulling a black Smith and Wesson .38 out of the large Perspex cube used to contain superglue fumes that polymerised the water and sebaceous deposits in fingerprints. It had been a month since I'd last been in a lab, but I felt immediately at home. The landscape of fingerprint science is the same no matter where you are—ninhydrin air; superglue residue flaking like old skin from the white Formica benchtops; the rattling beat of fume cupboard fans. I slipped on an off-white lab coat that was too long at the sleeves and covered in the purple and brown stains of sloppy chemistry.

Catherine placed the gun on a white sheet of butcher paper and rolled off her white plastic gloves. 'A dick from homicide goes to see what the local chickenhawk knows about a dead underage hooker. Chickenhawk gets nervous and pulls a gun. The cop wrestles control of the gun, but the guy screams it was the cop who drew the weapon. Check it out.' She nodded down at the gun.

I moved in beside her and peered down at the lines and curves the superglue had formed on the muzzle.

'The dick's prints are on the card by your elbow,' Catherine said.

I picked up the card and stared at Alex Pace's fingerprints.

'I tested the gun's butt and the muzzle. Cop's prints are on the muzzle, not the butt's grip. He's in the clear.'

But I was still staring at Alex's print card. 'These can't be right.'

She shrugged. 'I took them myself when he started.'

Only five percent of people have an arch as one of their ten patterns. Yet he had an arch on every finger on his right hand.

Catherine leaned back against the bench and looked over my shoulder at the card. 'Strange, aren't they?'

In the centre of his right thumb was an ulnar arch as sharp as the point of a blade. Ridges circled the pattern like waves in a pond rushing from the drop of a stone. His pointer was a plain arch with ridges that rose and met in the shape of a bullet. The index finger was a mixture of a loop and tented arch that merged to look like the letter 'S' laid horizontally. His ring finger was another plain arch as rounded as a handcuff's loop.

Catherine tapped a finger on the left side of the card. 'It gets weirder. The left hand classifications are your standard, dull old loops, but his papillary lines are the longest I've ever seen.'

Before fingerprinting was a science, elongated papillary ridges were seen as signs of passion. If hands lived a life of lust, it could be detected by the thrust of their lines. Professionally, we ignored these implications. Privately, we still peeked.

A man with one handful of pyramids and another of curves. The extraordinary and the ordinary in a single person.

She rolled her eyes. 'That's Alex for you.'

I stepped around her and peered down at the fine white ridges on the barrel of the gun. They were barely visible compared to the thick lines on the handle. 'His prints are light.'

'Tell me about it. It's taken me two days just to get them to show. A guy points a gun at me, I'd be sweating so much that my prints would glow in the dark.'

It was all those arches, I thought. Five examples of perfect balance and symmetry. All lines connecting. How could a man with five arches be anything but focused? He had obviously subdued the influence of the curves.

I waved his card in the air. 'If you're finished with this, I'll refile it.'

'Thanks.'

Using the edge of the butcher paper as a makeshift glove, Catherine pushed the gun into an open space on the bench and began setting up the equipment needed to photograph the prints on its barrel and butt.

On my way to the filing cabinets I stopped by the photocopy room. It was empty. I slipped Alex's record card into the machine and made a copy. I returned the original and discretely tucked the duplicate into the inside pocket of my bag.

Within a week I knew his every crease and curve. Each night I'd sit at my small pine desk with a jeweller's magnifier clamped to my left eye. Beneath the tungsten of my banker's lamp, I would search his patterns for clues about his life. The pucker of a scar on the right side of the highest ridge of his left index. The commonest spot for a cut from a cooking knife. He had to be right handed.

He had old man's hands. Ridges like grain in a timber plank, curves like the knots that sink in aging wood. Cutting across the ink on each fingerpad were the narrow, oval, white spaces made by creases in the epidermis. A lifetime of dry hands. Constant exposure to wind could sap a finger's moisture and leave the surface this cracked. So could frequent immersion in water. I wondered if he were an outdoor type. At the base of his thumbs was a roll of skin, an extra millimetre of flesh eased down the length of the finger by decades of gravity. It reminded me of the way medieval stained glass windows swell at the sill. He had to be at least thirty when the prints were taken.

I wished I could check for signs of love, but with a single set of prints, it was impossible. I needed an object he had touched. Love could only be detected through comparison and careful testing. Or so I had found. It was my theory that the swelling of the heart produces in the pores a mixture of minerals and acids different from those found in a normal fingerprint. There is more creatine and more uric acid, but fewer amino acids. Passion's sweat is so strong you never need to dust it with black powder or expose it by lumalight. Its mark is always visible, never latent. Love defines a fingerprint like a tattoo stains the skin.

I was wrong about him subduing the curves.

I finally met Alex two months later when I was called out on a cool spring morning to fingerprint the body of an eight-year-old boy found in the muddy Burnley backwash of the Yarra. October storms had swollen the river, its force a cannonball that had rolled the body into the duckweed shallows.

Peterson was supervising the removal of the body from the water. The mother was up on the bank, locked in the dimpled arms of a podgy cop with skin as sallow as boiling butter. Peterson's blunt instructions carried across the marshy plain and up to where the mother stood. I cringed as I heard him order the body be brought in with hooks. A bullet had turned the boy's chest into a rotting black hole.

A dark haired cop flew down the bank at us. When he reached our plateau I saw he was taller than Peterson, but also rounder. While Peterson's face and limbs were long planes, this man's were swelling lines. The controlled curves, I decided, of a man whose body wanted to be bigger than its master allowed.

'Hey, keep it down,' the man demanded. His eyes never left Peterson's face but Peterson's were everywhere. 'The last thing that woman up there needs is to hear you talking about her child like he's a side of beef.'

Peterson seemed like a coiled spring about to leap. He grabbed the flapping tie with his left hand and pinned it to his narrow chest. 'Get back up there, Pace. And why is the mother still hanging around?'

Pace. Alex Pace? I wanted to grab this tall man's hand and turn it over to examine the finger pads.

Pace's right hand clenched into a fist at his side and his left rose to rest on the slight curve of his hip. One arm a loop, the other an arch.

'She needs to see this for herself, or she'll always wonder what really happened to him.' Pace's voice was low and smooth but the tricep muscle of his right arm strained against his white overalls as his fist clenched even tighter. I realised his calmness was an effort.

Peterson threw his arms in the air. The tie flew back over his right shoulder again. 'Needs to see this? Since when do we let family see us picking over the bodies? You want her to watch the autopsy too?' He turned to me. 'After the other technicians are finished, you can print him here on the bank.'

I swung to face Peterson, my arms folded across my chest.

'I am not printing this kid in front of his mother,' I said. 'I don't care if I have to do it at the morgue at 3 a.m., just as long as she's not there to see it.' I turned to Alex. 'And I don't know what weird theory you're following, but to get this kid's prints, I have to slice off the skin on his hand and wear it like a glove. You understand me? Somehow I don't think that's going to help her grieve.'

I picked up my case and fled—from the boy with the hole of hate in his chest, from this detective whose fingers bore too many curves.

The next time I saw Alex I was browsing in a second hand bookstore on Barkly Street, St Kilda, a seven-minute tram ride from my office. I always came to St Kilda when I wanted to avoid running into the people I worked with. Through a fingerprinter's eyes, St Kilda was a place where thieves were either too smacked out to wear gloves or so stoned that they dropped them before escaping. We spent too many hours collecting easy prints in this suburb of decaying window sills, maze-like alleys and uncontrollable drugs to want to pass our leisure time here too. I had thought it would be the same for homicide detectives.

He was standing in the text-book section, flipping through a yellowing Oxford atlas. On its matt brown cover two children in orange trousers tossed a world globe between them. I remembered using the same book during my high school years back in Perth. The woody dust from old, cheap paper pulp breezed across the room at me each time he turned a page.

I had entered the shop simply to escape the geometry of the morning's work. I had been manually comparing each delta and bifurcation of a latent print found at a robbery the week before with the loops and whirls of the twenty matches the computer had selected. Unless I took my break in a place of uneven shapes, I would go line mad.

I tapped him on the shoulder.

He turned to face me. 'Sarah!'

He must have read my surprise at his knowing my name because he suddenly turned back to the book case and slipped the atlas between two similar sized volumes. When he faced me again, his cheeks were flushed.

'I'm Alex,' he said as he offered a hand.

'I remember.'

His hand was warm. I pictured the imprint of the curves, not the arches, on my skin, and then a coolness as they faded. Fingerprints on skin last only a few moments.

'How's the boy's mother?'

'Better.' It had been two months since his body had been found. 'I dropped in to see her yesterday.'

'The case is still open?'

He nodded and ran a hand through his hair. The curls were clipped now, ordered and controlled. 'I want to apologise about that day.'

I held up a hand as a signal to stop. 'You do your job well. That's all that matters.'

'So do you.' He cleared his throat. 'What time are you due back?'

I checked my watch. 'Another fifty minutes.'

'Have coffee with me?'

I smiled. 'Okay.'

Homicide's night shift met in the coffee room at 11.00 p.m. to assign cases and swap stories. At 11.15 that night I slipped upstairs to their floor with a pair of tweezers and a paper bag in my pocket.

There were sixteen desks in the workrooms, all cluttered but unmanned. I looked for signs of Alex in each. My eye lingered on one carrel two desks from the window that overlooked the sea. On it sat a wooden world globe used as a paperweight for a stack of blank report forms. I saw his thoroughness in the yellow highlighted sentences of interview transcripts, his kindness in a floral, thank-you card from a victim's sister. And on the top right corner of his desk, adhered with sticky tape, his sorrow in a school photograph of the blond haired, freckled boy we'd fished from the river.

I turned from these things and looked for something he would not miss. The piece of paper he'd hastily scribbled my phone number on was now a coaster for his dark blue, lacquered coffee mug. A thick ring of moisture had blurred the ink. The digits were now unreadable. A teledex sat by his phone. When I opened it to the entries beginning with 'S', I saw my name and number in black pen. I lifted the mug and used the pair of tweezers to transfer the piece of paper into the bag. I took it home to test for signs of emotion.

That was my heart's first theft.

Acknowledgements

A million thanks to
Professor Josie Arnold, Kitty Vigo and Dan Stainsby. A
more talented team there never was. Josie, you are a
guiding light whose sparkle helps so many others shine.

Endless appreciations to the following writers and critical
readers who shared their wisdom, talent and kindness
with me over the years: Delia Falconer, Sandy Webster,
Ania Walwicz, Laurie Clancy and Judy Duffy from RMIT;
Fiona Capp from LaTrobe University; Jacqueline Ross,
Peter Farnbach, and the very special Electra Ulrich for
their insightful and always helpful comments on my
manuscripts. Each of you have contributed to these
stories in your own unique ways.